Caroline

Illustrations by
Robin Davies and Jerry Smith

EGMONT

EGMONT

We bring stories to life

First published in Great Britain in 2007
by Egmont UK Limited
239 Kensington High Street, London W8 6SA
All Rights Reserved

Thomas the Tank Engine & Friends™

A BRITT ALLCROFT COMPANY PRODUCTION

Based on The Railway Series by The Reverend W Awdry
© 2007 Gullane (Thomas) LLC. A HIT Entertainment Company

Thomas the Tank Engine & Friends and Thomas & Friends are trademarks of Gullane (Thomas) Limited.
Thomas the Tank Engine & Friends and Design is Reg. US. Pat. & Tm. Off.

ISBN 978 1 4052 2937 1
1 3 5 7 9 10 8 6 4 2
Printed in Great Britain

The Forest Stewardship Council (FSC) is an international, non-governmental organisation
dedicated to promoting responsible management of the world's forests. FSC operates a
system of forest certification and product labelling that allows consumers to identify
wood and wood-based products from well managed forests.

For more information about Egmont's paper buying policy please visit www.egmont.co.uk/ethicalpublishing

For more information about the FSC please visit their website at www.fsc.uk.org

*T*his is a story about Caroline, a lazy car who thought she would never like engines. Then, one day, she found they could be Really Useful…

On a beautifully sunny day on the Island of Sodor, Caroline the car was sitting at the side of a cricket pitch. She was watching her owner play a very long game of cricket.

"What a pleasant day," thought Caroline.

Caroline liked to sit and watch people playing cricket because it meant they weren't hurtling about the countryside, revving her delicate engine, and going too fast.

Meanwhile, at the Transfer Yards, Stepney the Bluebell Engine, was chatting to the other engines.

"Trucks are fun," he was telling Percy.

Percy was very surprised. Surely no engines actually liked trucks? "Well, you can pull some of mine if you like," said Percy.

Percy's Driver agreed that Stepney could pull some of the trucks. Stepney was so happy, he set off around the Island with a big smile on his face.

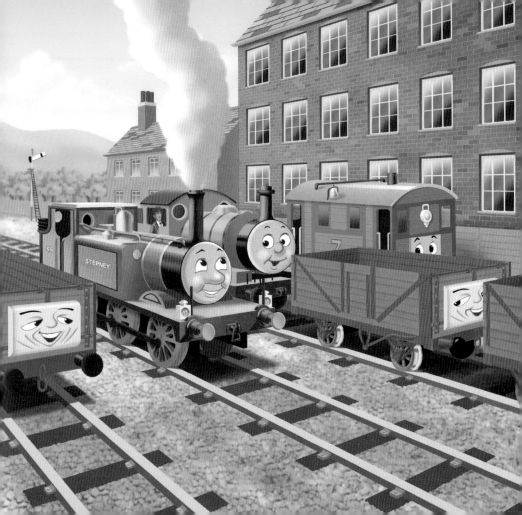

While Caroline was happily dozing in the sunshine, Stepney pulled up at a signal behind her.

Caroline didn't like engines very much; she thought they were silly because they liked to rush around too fast.

Suddenly, the batsman hit the ball. It flew high into the sky above Stepney.

"Clunk!" went the signal.

"Thump!" went the ball. And landed in a truck!

Neither Stepney nor his Driver noticed the ball land in one of Stepney's trucks.

"Come along," puffed Stepney, to the trucks.

"Stop!" shouted the players. "That's our only ball!"

"Wake up, Caroline!" called the players, as they clambered inside her cab. "Follow that train!"

Caroline coughed crossly and rolled down the road.

Stepney wasn't going very quickly and Caroline soon came up behind him.

"Toot, toot!" called Caroline. The players shouted but the Driver was too far away to hear them properly. He thought they wanted a race.

"Faster, Stepney!" shouted the Driver. And Stepney began to puff along very fast.

Poor Caroline! She wasn't happy at all. Her owner was making her go faster and faster!

As Caroline turned a corner, Stepney disappeared. "Hurrah!" she cried. "That silly train has fallen into a hole. I can go home now."

But Caroline's owner only made her go faster! He pushed her up a steep hill and down the other side.

As Caroline hurtled down the hill she could see Stepney sitting in a station at the bottom.

Caroline cluttered into the station. She was wheezing and coughing and spluttering. Caroline hoped Stepney wouldn't leave before the players got their ball back.

The players ran towards Stepney.
"Our ball," they cried. "Where's our ball?"

The Driver looked very confused. "Your ball?" he asked. "Why would we have your ball?"

The players explained everything as they began to search in Stepney's trucks. The trucks were wriggling and jiggling making it harder for the players to look.

"Stop it!" Stepney told the naughty trucks.

"Found it!" cried a player. "Let's get back to the game."

Stepney looked at Caroline. She was worn out. Stepney didn't think Caroline would want to drive anywhere.

Stepney spoke to his Driver. "Do you think we could give Caroline a lift?" he asked. "She looks very tired and I don't think she can make it back to the cricket pitch."

Stepney's Driver thought that was a splendid idea. He spoke to the Stationmaster and the Signalman.

"Stepney has had an idea," he explained. "Can you think of a way we could give Caroline a lift?"

Very soon they had a plan and were busily explaining it to the players.

Caroline wasn't too happy with the plan. She felt very nervous riding on a truck on the railway line.

"Just you be careful," she said to Stepney. "Don't go too fast, please."

"I'll be careful," promised Stepney.

Stepney uncoupled all of his trucks apart from a flat truck. Caroline was rolled on to the flat truck and a brake van was hooked up behind. The players all climbed on board.

Stepney began to pull out of the station.

Caroline had her eyes tightly shut.
"Ooooh!" she cried.

Slowly, Caroline noticed that she wasn't being shaken about at all. She opened her eyes to find that Stepney was going quite fast.

Caroline looked around the countryside.
She realised that she didn't mind going fast, especially when somebody else was doing all the work!

Stepney safely returned Caroline, and all the players, to the cricket pitch.

Stepney's Driver, the Stationmaster and Signalman settled down to watch the match.

"Perhaps engines aren't so silly, after all," said Caroline to Stepney. "They can certainly save the wear on a poor car's tyres!"

The Thomas Story Library is THE definitive collection of stories about Thomas and ALL his Friends.

5 more Thomas Story Library titles will be chuffing into your local bookshop in August 2007:

Rocky
Rosie
Dennis
Alfie
The Fat Controller

And there are even more
Thomas Story Library books to follow later!
So go on, start your Thomas Story Library NOW!

TO BE COMPLETED BY AN ADULT

To apply for this great offer, ask an adult to complete the coupon below and send it with a pound coin and 6 tokens, to:
THOMAS OFFERS, PO BOX 715, HORSHAM RH12 5WG

☐ Please send a Thomas poster and door hanger. I enclose 6 tokens plus a £1 coin. (Price includes P&P)

Fan's name..

Address...

....Postcode..............................

Date of birth..

Name of parent/guardian...

Signature of parent/guardian..

Please allow 28 days for delivery. Offer is only available while stocks last. We reserve the right to change the terms of this offer at any time and we offer a 14 day money back guarantee. This does not affect your statutory rights.

☐ Data Protection Act: If you do not wish to receive other similar offers from us or companies we recommend, please tick this box. Offers apply to UK only.

Cut along the dotted line